For Kristin, my unicorn

Copyright © 2019 by Scholastic Inc.

All rights reserved. Published by Scholastic Inc., *Publishers since 1920*. SCHOLASTIC and associated logos are trademarks and/or registered trademarks of Scholastic Inc.

The publisher does not have any control over and does not assume any responsibility for author or third-party websites or their content.

No part of this publication may be reproduced, stored in a retrieval system, or transmitted in any form or by any means, electronic, mechanical, photocopying, recording, or otherwise, without written permission of the publisher. For information regarding permission, write to Scholastic Inc., Attention: Permissions Department, 557 Broadway, New York, NY 10012.

This book is a work of fiction. Names, characters, places, and incidents are either the product of the author's imagination or are used fictitiously, and any resemblance to actual persons, living or dead, business establishments, events, or locales is entirely coincidental.

ISBN 978-1-338-56541-6

10 9 8 7 6 5 4 3   19 20 21 22 23

Printed in the U.S.A.   40
First printing 2019

Book design by Mercedes Padró
Edited by Jeremy West

Grumpy Unicorn

WhY me?

Joey Spiotto

Scholastic Inc.

Table of Contents

Part One
Meet Grumpy Unicorn
6

Part Two
All Year Round
40

Part One

Meet Grumpy Unicorn

Things Unicorns Love:

1. ~~Cupcakes~~
2. ~~Rainbows~~
3. ~~Glitter~~
4. ~~Hugs~~
5. ~~Bubble Baths~~
6. ~~Candy~~
7. ~~Ice Cream~~

Things Grumpy Unicorn Hates . . .

Magic tricks

Rainbows

Ice cream

Donuts

Slides

Bubble baths

Balloon animals

Hula-hoops

Unicycles

Busking

Topiary

Bowling

Piñatas

Crying

Allergy season

The Horse's Hoof

Shoe shopping

Shopping List

-Corn on the Cob
-Candy Corn
-Cornstarch
-Corn Bread
-Corn Chips
-Popcorn
-Corn Dogs

How to Spend
the Weekend:

Catch up with old friends

Go on an adventure

Eat a healthy snack

zzzz

Read a good book

Exercise

Clean the house

Grumpy Unicorn
Tries to Look Tough

Grumpy Unicorn
Gets a Haircut

Part Two

All
Year
Round

How to be Healthy:

Do sit-ups every day

Go for a run
(to the mailbox)

Lift weights

Jump rope

Do push-ups

Play basketball

Go for a swim

Make a healthy smoothie

Grumpy Valentine's Day

Grumpy St. Patrick's Day

Grumpy Easter

Grumpy Fourth of July

Grumpy Halloween

Grumpy Thanksgiving

Things I'm Thankful for:

1. Pumpkin Pie

2. Apple Pie

3. Pecan Pie

4. Sweet Potato Pie

5. Chocolate Cream Pie

6. Butterscotch Pie

7. Lemon Pie

8. Any Pie

9. Leftover Pie

A Very
Grumpy Christmas

Spring

Summer

Winter

Part Three

On
Vacation

A Day at the Beach

click

A Day at the Carnival

MUST BE THIS TALL TO RIDE

The sign reads: *Unicorn Cakes*

A Day at the Zoo

DO NOT FEED THE **LIONS**

Part Four

Time to Celebrate

Bad Birthday Gifts:

How to throw a Party:

1. Pick a date

2. Invite your friends

3. Make a playlist

1. ~~"If You're Happy and You Know It"~~
2. ~~"Happy Birthday to You"~~
3. "Don't Worry, Be ~~Happy~~" grumpy
4. ~~"Happy Trails to You"~~

4. Have plenty of snacks

5. Clean up before guests arrive

6. Make your guests a nice homemade meal

7. Decorate

8. Take a nap

9. Forget all about the party

10. Go on vacation

ABOUT THE AUTHOR

Joey Spiotto is an author, illustrator, and creator behind *Alien Next Door*, *Firefly Back From the Black*, and the print series Storytime. His artwork is regularly featured at the world-famous *Gallery 1988* in Los Angeles, CA, and he has previously worked on films, video games, clothing design, toys, and more. He lives just outside of Los Angeles with his wife and two boys, but you can visit him online at jo3bot.com.